THE NUTCRACKER

THE NUTCRACKER

Retold from
E.T.A. Hoffman
By Jane B. Mason

SCHOLASTIC INC.

This book is a work of fiction. Names, characters, places, and incidents are either the product of the author's imagination or are used fictitiously, and any resemblance to actual persons, living or dead, business establishments, events, or locales is entirely coincidental.

No part of this publication may be reproduced, stored in a retrieval system, or transmitted in any form or by any means, electronic, mechanical, photocopying, recording, or otherwise, without written permission of the publisher.
For information regarding permission, write to Scholastic Inc., Attention: Permissions Department, 557 Broadway, New York, NY 10012.

ISBN 978-0-439-44604-4

The publisher does not have any control over and does not assume any responsibility for author or third-party websites or their content.

12 11 10 9 8 7 6 5 4 3 2 1   17 18 19 20 21 22

Printed in the U.S.A.   40

This edition first printing, November 2017

Contents

THE NUTCRACKER

Christmas Eve

MARIE Stahlbaum and her older brother, Fritz, could barely contain their excitement. What wonderful gifts were waiting for them under the giant Christmas tree? What glorious decorations covered the tree's branches?

Since they were not allowed into the parlor, they did not know. All day long they sat and waited. They heard strange murmuring and shuffling, pounding and hammering. And late in the afternoon, Fritz declared that he saw a familiar, strange-looking man creep into the parlor with a large box under his arm.

Marie's eyes lit up with excitement. "That's Godfather Drosselmeier!" she exclaimed. "Oooh, I wonder what marvelous toy he has made for us this year?"

Fritz and Marie were fortunate children. Every year their parents gave them and their older sister, Louise, lovely Christmas gifts. But the most glorious gift always came from Godfather Drosselmeier.

Godfather Drosselmeier was a skilled clockmaker and craftsman. Whenever one of the clocks at the Stahlbaums' home was sick and unable to strike properly, Godfather Drosselmeier came to fix it.

When Marie was very young, the sight of Godfather Drosselmeier scared her, for he was not a handsome man. He was short and had skinny legs. His face was wrinkled and creased. He wore a patch where his right eye should have been. And under his white wig, which stuck out at crazy angles, he did not have a single hair on his head.

When Marie got older, she learned that Godfather Drosselmeier was a sweet and wonderful man in spite of his strange looks. And she always looked forward to the amazing creations he brought at Christmas.

"I hope he's made us a fortress," Fritz said loudly. "One with all kinds of soldiers ready for battle."

Marie shook her head. "Oh, no," she said firmly. She was used to disagreeing with her brother. "Godfather Drosselmeier once told me about a beautiful castle with gardens and a lake with swans —"

"Who cares about swans?" Fritz replied rudely. "And anyway, Godfather Drosselmeier's presents always get put in the cabinet before we have a chance to do anything fun with them. At least we get to do what we want with the presents Mother and Father give us."

Marie didn't reply, because she was too busy wondering what might be under the tree for her. She hoped it was a new doll, for Marie loved dolls.

"Father knows I need a chestnut horse

for my royal stables and a cavalry for my army," Fritz announced. "Then I would be able to have a proper battle."

And so the children waited, wondering what lay in store for them. Finally, just after dark, a bell rang, *ding-a-ling!* The parlor doors flew open and the children, who had crept as close to the parlor as possible, were bathed in bright light.

"Oh!" they exclaimed in surprise. Fritz's and Marie's eyes widened at the glorious sight of the Christmas tree — and the presents beneath it.

The tree stood in the middle of the large parlor and was decorated with all kinds of tantalizing treats. There were apples and sugared nuts and gumdrops. Shiny red and gold ornaments hung from the silvery-green branches. And tiny white candles were nestled in the boughs, lighting up the tree like sunrise.

Beneath the tree were presents as far as

the eye could see. There were so many that nobody dared to try to count them.

Dr. and Mrs. Stahlbaum laughed as their children rushed into the room, shrieking and shouting for joy.

Marie hurried forward and picked an apple from the tree. It was juicy and sweet. Kneeling down, she found several beautiful dolls to play with, including a large one in a fine outfit. And there was a fancy silk dress decorated with colorful ribbons.

"How lovely!" she cried again and again.

Meanwhile, Fritz had discovered his chestnut horse (complete with bridle) and was busily galloping around the room on its back.

"He's a little wild," Fritz announced when he had finished the ride. "But I'm sure I'll be able to break him." He set the horse down and began to play with his little Russian soldiers. They were smartly dressed, with red-and-gold uniforms and silver swords. They even had white horses to carry them into battle!

Fritz and Marie spent several hours playing with their dolls, horses, and soldiers. Then they sat down to read through some of the picture books their mother and father had given them. The books were full of beautiful paintings of flowers and faraway places and children playing.

Suddenly, the Christmas bell rang again. Jumping to their feet, the children ran to a table set up in the corner of the room. It was time to unveil Godfather Drosselmeier's latest creation.

Marie's eyes filled with light as the screen hiding Godfather's gift was pulled aside. There, sitting on the table, was the most enchanting castle she had ever seen.

The castle sparkled like gold and had dozens of shiny glass windows and glimmering spires. The doors and windows opened and closed, revealing handsomely dressed ladies and gentlemen strolling about the rooms. In the large front hall, silver chandeliers were ablaze with candles. Children in little skirts danced to chimes that played. A man dressed in an emerald cloak kept appearing and disappearing at one of the windows. And a figure that looked exactly like Godfather Drosselmeier himself occasionally came out of the castle to stand at the garden gate before going back inside again.

Marie listened intently to the chimes and watched the lovely figures move about. The castle was truly magical!

But Fritz did not think so. He wanted to be able to step inside the castle himself. Or at the very least, he wanted the figures to do something different.

"That is impossible," Godfather Drosselmeier said. "The figures can only do what they are designed to do and nothing more."

Fritz let out a bored sigh. "Well that's not very interesting, is it?" he said. "I prefer my soldiers, who march back and forth as I command. They aren't shut up in a silly castle."

Godfather Drosselmeier scowled at Fritz and began to pack up his castle. But Marie and her mother asked him to show them what made the people move, and he excitedly took the castle apart to show them. Then he put it back together again just in time for dinner.

2.

The Nutcracker

EVERYONE except Marie left the parlor for the dining room. You see, Marie had spied something else under the tree. She hadn't seen it before, since Fritz's soldiers had been parading back and forth, blocking her view. She wanted a chance to look at it carefully and by herself.

It was an excellent little man in a red soldier's jacket, complete with gold buttons. His breeches were of the same fabric, and on his feet he wore dainty little boots. He seemed to be waiting patiently under the evergreen boughs for someone to notice him.

Marie picked up the little man and held him close. As she gazed at him she realized that he was rather funny looking. His head was much larger than the rest of him. His body was too long. His legs were extremely skinny. And over his smart uniform he wore a skimpy cloak that looked as though it was made of wood.

"Never mind," Marie told the little man. "Godfather Drosselmeier often wears an ugly cloak and cap, and he is still my kind, sweet godfather."

She gazed down at the little man's face and noticed his kind green eyes, his bright-red lips, and his white cotton beard. "And you are much handsomer than he," Marie added in a whisper.

Happily carrying her new doll, Marie made her way to the dinner table.

"Father," she asked, "to whom does this dear little man belong?"

Dr. Stahlbaum looked over at the man Marie was holding. "Our friend belongs to you and Louise and Fritz. He will serve you well, cracking hard nuts for you with his teeth."

Marie's father picked up the toy and lifted his wooden cloak. The little man opened his mouth wide, and the children could see two rows of sharp teeth inside. Marie slipped a nut inside. *CRACK!* The shell split in two and the nut meat fell into Marie's outstretched hand.

"Our little friend is descended from the Nutcracker family. He has learned his trade well from his ancestors. I am sure he will serve all of you very nicely."

Marie laughed and clapped her hands in delight.

"Since you are so fond of our friend Nutcracker, he shall be entrusted to your care," Dr. Stahlbaum said. "But remember, he belongs to Fritz and Louise as much as you."

"Oh, thank you, Father," Marie said. She sat down and placed Nutcracker next to her at the dinner table. During the course of the meal he was passed around, cracking nuts for the whole family. Marie always chose the smallest nuts so Nutcracker would not have to open his mouth too wide. He seemed grateful, for he smiled and smiled at her.

Louise and her parents were also gentle with Nutcracker. But Fritz chose the biggest and hardest nuts. He jammed the wooden cloak down hard and — *crack, crack, crack* — three little teeth fell out of Nutcracker's jaw.

"You brute!" Marie scolded. "You've hurt him!"

Marie took Nutcracker from her brother's grasp and held him lovingly. "My poor Nutcracker! Don't worry, I'll take care of you."

"He's just a silly fool," Fritz announced. "What kind of Nutcracker has lousy teeth? Give him to me, Marie. I'll have him crack nuts until all his teeth fall out and his jaw drops off, too."

"No!" Marie shouted, practically in tears. "He's my special Nutcracker and you can't have him. Because of you he's looking at me sadly and showing me his sore mouth." She picked up Nutcracker's broken teeth and bandaged his jaw with a pretty white ribbon from her dress. Then she rocked Nutcracker like a baby so he wouldn't look so sad and pale.

3

Strange Events

THAT night, Marie and Fritz stayed up late, playing with their new things. Marie showed Nutcracker the beautiful pictures in her books. Then she set to work arranging her dolls in the cabinet.

The Stahlbaum children had a very large and beautiful glass cabinet that stood in the parlor. The cabinet had been made years and years before, and the cabinetmaker who made it was terribly skilled and clever. He'd chosen the finest and most sparkling glass for the door panels. Whatever was placed in the cabinet looked almost more beautiful and enchanting than it did when you played with it.

This gorgeous cabinet housed most of the Stahlbaum children's toys. On the very highest shelf were the spectacular toys that Godfather Drosselmeier had created. The shelf below that was full of picture books. The next shelf down served as the quarters for Fritz's troops. And the very lowest shelf was where Marie's dolls lived.

Marie had created a lovely home for her dolls. They had a flowered sofa for resting, several chairs, a tea table, and a comfortable bed to sleep in. The walls were decorated with colored pictures. It was a pleasant place to live, and the dolls were grateful.

Marie's favorite new doll was named Mistress Clara. She was ever so fancy in her dress decorated with fine ribbons. Indeed, it was fancier than Marie's own frock. Marie moved her old doll, Mistress Trude, out of the room for the time being and made everything comfortable for Clara. Then she set the tiny tea table, and she and Clara shared delicious tea and cakes.

By now it was getting late, and Mrs. Stahlbaum suggested that Fritz and Marie should go to bed. But the children were very excited about their Christmas toys and convinced her that it would be all right to play a while longer. Eventually, though, Fritz decided that his weary troops would do well with some rest. He placed them in the glass cabinet and went to bed.

Marie begged her mother to let her stay up just a bit longer. After putting out all the candles on the tree and around the cabinet, Mrs. Stahlbaum agreed. "But you should go to bed soon, or you won't be able to get up in the morning," she warned. Then she went off to bed.

Marie watched her mother go. As soon as she was out of sight, she picked Nut-cracker up off her lap, where he had been sitting all evening long. She gently laid

16

him on a table, untied her ribbon from his jaw, and checked his wounds carefully.

"Sweet Nutcracker," Marie said softly, "don't be angry at Fritz. He is a rough boy but does not mean to be bad. And I'm going to take care of you until you're perfectly well again."

Nutcracker gave Marie a sad smile. His face was still terribly pale.

Marie picked up Nutcracker and carried him back to the cabinet. "Mistress Clara," she said, "I'm going to ask you to give up your bed for our friend Nutcracker. Your round and rosy cheeks tell us how healthy you are, and poor Nutcracker needs his rest. The sofa should be just fine for you, since it is nice and soft."

Mistress Clara didn't say a word, but Marie thought she saw her glare jealously at Nutcracker.

"Never mind," said Marie. She pulled the bed out of the cabinet and laid Nutcracker on it. After pulling the covers up

17

to Nutcracker's nose, she set the bed on the shelf with Fritz's troops.

"I'm sure the soldiers won't mind sharing their quarters with an injured man," she said. With a satisfied smile, Marie closed the cabinet door and started off to bed.

Before Marie had crossed the room, a soft shuffling filled the air. It came from everywhere at once — behind the sofa, inside the walls, and under the floor. The tall clock began to whir and whir, louder and louder, but it did not strike. Looking up, Marie saw that the owl perched on top of the clock had dropped its wings down over the clock face. Suddenly, the clock began to speak!

"All clocks must now stop ticking.
Make no sound, hold your striking,
The Mouse King hears the tiniest
    clicking,

Purr, purr, poom, poom,
Tonight may be the night of doom."

Marie shivered and was about to flee when she spied Godfather Drosselmeier. He was sitting on top of the clock! The owl was gone, and Godfather Drosselmeier's yellow coattails hung over the clock like giant wings.

"Godfather Drosselmeier!" Marie called out. "Come down off that clock and stop frightening me so!"

But before Godfather Drosselmeier could reply, a rather loud squeaking noise filled the room. There was a great scratching sound, and hundreds of mice appeared. They squeezed between floorboards and through cracks in the walls. They kept coming and coming, until they practically filled the room. Their beady little eyes looked like tiny green lights.

The mice scrambled into a special formation, and Marie realized that she was witnessing a mouse army forming ranks.

Unlike many children, Marie was not afraid of mice. As she watched them now she was not filled with fear, but curiosity — until a horrible squeaking noise bounced off the walls, sending shivers down her spine.

Before Marie could react, sand and crushed stone came spewing out of the floor. Then the most horrid creature imaginable rose up.

It was the hideous seven-headed Mouse King.

The mouse army cheered loudly for its king, letting out a chorus of squeaks. And then they began to march forward — straight toward Marie and the toy cabinet!

Marie began to feel faint. Just as the first row of mice reached her, she fell backward. *Crash!* Her arm broke through the cabinet door, splintering a glass panel.

For a moment, Marie felt a stinging

pain. Then it was gone. So, it seemed, were the mice, for she could no longer hear scampering or squeaking.

Instead, she heard someone speaking:

"Come, awake, arms to take,
Out to the fight, out to the fight.
Shield the left, shield the right.
Arm and away, this is the night."

A strange glow was coming from inside the toy cabinet! Marie looked up and saw all the dolls and soldiers and toys rushing around frantically. Nutcracker leaped out of bed and drew his sword.

"My friends and brothers, will you stand by me in this bitter battle?" he shouted.

"Yes, yes!" the dolls, soldiers, and other toys cried.

One by one they leaped down from their shelves. Poor Nutcracker couldn't jump! His wooden body was too brittle to take the fall. He paced back and forth, shouting orders to his troops. Then he stopped, looked over the edge, and jumped. . . .

Thud! Nutcracker landed safely in Mistress Clara's arms.

"My dear Clara!" Marie shouted in relief. "I am sorry to have doubted you. I'm certain now that you were perfectly willing to give Nutcracker your bed."

Mistress Clara didn't reply. She was too busy hugging Nutcracker to her breast. "My lord, please do not go into battle tonight. You need to rest with me instead, looking down on your victory from the brim of my feathered hat."

Nutcracker wriggled himself free of Clara's grasp, then knelt before her. "My lady, I shall remember your kindness toward me as I fight this night."

Clara held out a fancy ribbon from her dress, but Nutcracker would not take it. He gestured to the ribbon he already wore — the one from Marie's simple frock.

Then, with a heavy sigh, Nutcracker lifted his sword into the air and gracefully leaped from the lowest shelf onto the floor. It was time for the battle to begin.

4

The Battle

BANNERS flew. Bands played. Marie watched as toy after toy, soldier after soldier, formed ranks in the middle of the room. Then out came Fritz's weaponry — guns, muskets, and cannonballs.

Boom! The first shots were fired. Sugar balls flew into the army of mice, momentarily blinding the creatures. Then larger guns began to fire jawbreakers — *poom, poom, poom, poom* — one after another. Several mice were knocked down.

But the mice kept coming. They scurried over the guns and bit into the dolls. They used slingshots to fire tiny silver pills at the doll army.

It was chaos all around as the room filled with dust, mouse fur, and doll stuffing from the battle.

And then, above the noise, a loud voice cried out. It was Mistress Clara.

"I am too beautiful to die!" she shouted from the safety of the toy cabinet.

The armies ignored her. *Crash! Boom! Bang!* The battle raged on. Nutcracker strode through the front lines, barking orders.

"Advance!" he shouted. And then, "Aim, fire!" But he didn't see the mice charging.

"*Squeeeeak!*" They rushed the jawbreaker cannons, knocking over the footstool they rested on and a dozen soldiers along with it.

Nutcracker surveyed the battlefield. Things did not look good. His troops fought with great determination, but the mice just kept coming.

A fierce mouse captain hurled himself forward and bit the head off of a brave emperor. Though the mouse choked on the emperor's stuffing and died, Nutcracker's troops began to lose heart.

"Bring up the reserves!" Nutcracker bellowed. A last few soldiers emerged from the toy cabinet, but they lacked skill and weaponry. Indeed, the first thing the soldiers did was knock General Nutcracker's cap to the floor. It was not long before the mice had bitten off the reserve troops' legs. They toppled, knocking over even more of the doll army.

Now Nutcracker was surrounded. He tried to jump back into the toy cabinet, but his wooden legs were not long enough. Clara had fainted on the floor. Soldiers rushed past their commander into the cabinet, fleeing for their lives.

In the mayhem, a pair of mice grabbed Nutcracker, and the horrible Mouse King charged. It seemed all was lost.

"Oh, my poor, poor Nutcracker!" Marie cried. Desperate, she removed her left shoe and hurled it as hard as she could at the Mouse King. As soon as she did so, everything disappeared. Marie's left arm throbbed painfully and all went black.

5

The Invalid

WHEN Marie finally awoke, she found herself in her own cozy bed. Sun was streaming through her windows, and the outsides of the panes were covered with beautiful frost-flowers.

Dr. Wendelstern was sitting beside her. "She's awake," he said gently to Marie's mother.

In an instant, Mrs. Stahlbaum was at her daughter's side, looking Marie over very anxiously.

"Oh, Mother!" Marie cried. "Are the horrible mice gone? Is Nutcracker safe?"

Marie's mother frowned. "Don't talk nonsense, child," she said. "It was very naughty of you to stay up so late. You cut your arm on the glass-paneled cabinet, and Dr. Wendelstern says you nearly ended up with a useless left limb. Thank goodness I woke at midnight and came looking for you. You were lying in front of the cabinet, bleeding frightfully. Fritz's soldiers and several broken toys were scattered around you. Nutcracker lay on your bleeding arm, and your left shoe was halfway across the parlor."

"Oh, Mother," Marie said in a hushed voice. "That was the evidence of a huge battle between the dolls and the mice. The mice were about to capture poor Nutcracker, so I threw my shoe at the terrible Mouse King. That is the last thing I remember."

Dr. Wendelstern looked meaningfully at Marie's mother.

"It's all right, child," Mrs. Stahlbaum said gently. "The mice are gone and Nutcracker is safe and sound in the toy cabinet."

Marie felt better when she heard that Nutcracker was safe. But she still had to stay in bed and take medicine for several days. And her arm was very sore and achy, which made it hard to do things.

Marie was very bored sitting in bed all day long. But in the evenings, her mother sat with her and told wonderful stories. She had just finished the one about Prince Fardarkin when the door opened and Godfather Drosselmeier burst in.

"I must see with my own eyes how my little Marie is getting along," he said. His yellow coattails flapped behind him as he came into the room.

Marie looked at those coattails and shrieked. "Oh, Godfather, how awful you were!" she said. "I saw you cover the clock to prevent it from striking and scaring away the mice. I heard you call the Mouse King. And why didn't you help Nut-cracker? It's all your fault that I cut myself and have to lie here in bed."

Mrs. Stahlbaum's eyes widened in alarm. Godfather Drosselmeier made all kinds of strange faces. Then he began to chant:

"Pendulum could only whisper,
Couldn't tick, not even a click;
All clocks stopped their ticking,
Then struck loud, dong, bong!
Dolls, don't let your heads hang down,
Bells are ringing! The battle is over!
Nutcracker is oh so safe in clover.
Here's the owl, on downy wing,
Come to scare the Mouse King.
Pendulum swing, and tick and click,
Brrr and purr, whir and stir."

Marie stared at Godfather Drosselmeier in fright, because he looked even stranger than usual. His arms were jerking about as if he were a puppet!

Before Marie could ask him to stop, Fritz came in and began to laugh. "Goodness, Godfather Drosselmeier," he said. "You are being very funny today. You make me think of the jumping jack that I just threw away."

Mrs. Stahlbaum looked quite concerned. "That certainly is a strange way to go on," she said. "What is the meaning of it?"

"Did you never hear my watchmaker's song?" Godfather Drosselmeier replied with a laugh. Then he sat down on Marie's bed.

"Don't be angry with me for not gouging out all of the Mouse King's fourteen eyes," he said. "That would have been quite impossible. But to make up for it, I have something you will enjoy a great deal."

And with that he reached into his pocket and pulled out Nutcracker! His jaw was nicely mended and his teeth had been put back in.

Marie took Nutcracker and hugged him tightly.

"Now you can see how good Godfather Drosselmeier is to your Nutcracker," Mrs. Stahlbaum said.

Godfather Drosselmeier nodded at Marie. "Even nicely mended," he said, "you must admit that Nutcracker is not at all handsome. If you like, I can tell you how the ugliness came into his family. Have you ever heard of Princess Pirlipat, Witch Mouserinks, and the clever clockmaker?"

Fritz interrupted. "Say, Godfather Drosselmeier, what happened to Nutcracker's sword? You've repaired him quite nicely, but what's become of his sword?"

Godfather Drosselmeier seemed annoyed by Fritz's question. "Why must you always complain, boy?" he asked. "I've mended his body; he'll have to find his own sword."

"Right," Fritz agreed. "If he's a worthy chap, he'll find a good weapon."

"So, Marie," Godfather Drosselmeier

repeated, "have you heard the story of Princess Pirlipat?"

"Oh, no!" Marie said. "Oh, please tell it, Godfather Drosselmeier!"

Mrs. Stahlbaum looked a bit anxious. "I hope it isn't as horrid as your stories generally are."

"On the contrary, dear lady," said Godfather Drosselmeier. "This is a fairy tale."

The Story of the Hard Nut

MARIE settled back against her pillows and Godfather Drosselmeier began to tell the tale.

❧ ❧ ❧

From the moment she was born, Pirlipat was a princess. For you see, her mother was a queen and her father was a king. The king was overjoyed with his lovely daughter as she lay in her cradle. He danced and hopped about, singing: "Hurrah! Hurrah! Has anyone ever seen something as lovely as my little Pirlipat?"

And all of his ministers, generals, presidents, and officers hopped about and replied: "No! Not ever!"

Indeed, Princess Pirlipat was a beautiful girl. Her tiny face looked as though it had been woven from delicate, rose-colored silk. Her big blue eyes were the color of azure stones. Her hair curled like golden threads. And she was born with two rows of pearly white teeth, which she put to use almost immediately. Two hours after she was born, she bit the lord high chancellor's finger. This may have caused some alarm if Pirlipat were a normal little girl. However, the entire kingdom was thrilled with this event. They felt it clearly showed that the tiny princess was not only beautiful but intelligent and spirited as well.

While the king and his kingdom were filled with joy over little Pirlipat, the queen seemed uneasy. She required that little Pirlipat's cradle be constantly and closely guarded. Guards were stationed at the nursery doors. Two head nurses kept watch at the cradle. And six additional nurses were positioned around the room at night, each holding a large tomcat on her lap. What's more, each of these nurses was required to pet the tomcat all night long so that it never ceased purring.

Nobody quite understood why these precautions were necessary. But I know why, and I shall tell you now.

Not long before, there was a large gathering of kings and princes at little Pirlipat's father's court. The king planned great entertainments, including tournaments, plays, and balls. He also planned a magnificent feast of puddings and sausages.

Then he rode out in his carriage and personally invited the kings and princes to attend his supper, which, he fibbed, would be "a simple soup," and nothing more.

Upon returning home, the king went to his wife and said, "Only you, my dear, know exactly how I like my puddings and sausages."

The queen, who understood her husband quite well, knew that he intended for her to make the puddings and sausages herself. Since she enjoyed being in the kitchen and loved her husband, she agreed.

The great golden sausage kettle was brought out of storage, along with the silver casseroles. The ladies-in-waiting built a crackling sandalwood fire. And the queen put on her damask apron.

Very shortly after that, the succulent aroma of pudding broth drifted throughout the castle. The king was so drawn to the smell that he excused himself from the council room and dashed into the kitchen. There he embraced his wife and spent a few divine moments stirring the broth himself. Calmed by the aroma and the stirring motion, he returned to work.

Soon there came the critical time when the meat was to be cut into small pieces and browned on silver spits. The ladies-in-waiting retired, for the queen had decided to do this task alone. But as soon as the meat began to sizzle, a voice was heard in the great palace kitchen.

"Give me some of that, sister!" the voice said. "I want some, and I am a queen as well as you."

The queen knew exactly who was speaking. It was Madame Mouserinks. Madame Mouserinks had lived in the castle for many years and claimed to be of royal blood. She was queen of Mousolia for certain and had her own large congregation under the stove.

Although the queen did not admit to being related to Madame Mouserinks, she was a kindly woman. "Come out then," she said. "Of course I will share my meat with you."

Madame Mouserinks wasted no time in scurrying out from under the stove. She greedily gobbled down every piece of meat that the good queen handed to her.

Then she called her aunts and uncles and cousins and five no-good sons, who all came out to share in the feast.

The queen was so overwhelmed by the number of mice that she could not keep them from eating all the meat. Luckily, one of the ladies-in-waiting came into the kitchen and shooed the mice back under the stove.

There was very little meat left for the king's sausages — so little that the court mathematician was called in to carefully calculate how to divide the meat so as to stretch it as far as possible.

Finally, the preparations were complete. Kings and princes arrived, dressed in their finest robes. The king greeted them and they all sat down to supper. Wearing his crown and sitting at the head of the table, the king tasted the first course. No sooner had the first bite passed his lips than his skin paled and he turned his eyes to the heavens. Then the second course was served. After taking a single bite, he broke down and sobbed, woefully covering his face with his hands.

The court physician rushed to the king's side and took the king's pulse. He began to apply very serious and powerful remedies. No one was sure what ailed the king so terribly, but it seemed to be gnawing at his very soul.

Then, suddenly, the king seemed to recover somewhat, for he uttered three words: "Too little meat."

The queen knelt at his feet in despair, crying. "Oh, my poor husband! What torture you have endured this day. The culprit is here at your feet — Madame Mouserinks, with her cousins and aunts and uncles and five sons, ate nearly all the meat. . . ." And before she could go on, the queen fell to the floor in a faint.

The king seemed to have regained his

senses, for he now jumped up in a rage. "Chief lady-in-waiting," he cried, "what is the meaning of this?"

The lady-in-waiting told the king what she knew, and the king vowed revenge on Madame Mouserinks and her family. The privy council was summoned, and it was decided that Madame Mouserinks should be tried for her life. Her property was confiscated. The king, however, worried that in spite of this she might continue to eat the sausage meat. So he turned the matter over to the court clockmaker.

This man's name was the same as mine — Christian Elias Drosselmeier. He promised to drive Madame Mouserinks and all of her relations from the palace forever. What he did, in fact, was to invent tiny machines and attach small pieces of cheese to them. He placed them all over Madame Mouserink's dwelling.

Madame Mouserinks was far too clever

to let herself get caught in one of these traps. But though she warned her aunts and uncles and cousins and sons, they could not resist the bits of cheese. Each time they nibbled a delicious morsel, they were trapped by a tiny gate, taken to the kitchen, and duly executed!

Madame Mouserinks was filled with despair and rage at her loss. While the king and his kingdom rejoiced, the queen knew they had not heard the last of the shrewd queen of Mousolia. And she was right. For Madame Mouserinks appeared before the queen as she was cooking her husband a chicken fricassee.

"My sons and my uncles, my cousins and my aunts are gone. Be warned, lady, that the queen of mice just might bite your little princess in two. Be warned!"

Then Madame Mouserinks vanished. The queen was so frightened that she dropped the fricassee in the fire, which made the king very angry. This was the second time Madame Mouserinks had ruined one of his favorite meals.

❧❦ ❧❦ ❧❦

Godfather Drosselmeier cleared his throat then and declared that the children had heard enough for one night. And though Marie begged him to continue, he refused.

7

Revenge

THE next evening, Godfather Drossel-meier returned to Marie's bedside and continued the story.

❧ ❧ ❧

Now you understand why the queen had her daughter guarded so carefully. She knew in her heart that Madame Mouserinks would eventually follow through on her threat. But the court astronomer declared that Tomcat Purr and his brothers would be able to keep the clever mouse witch away from the cradle.

And so they did, for a time. But one night, just after the clock struck twelve, one of the ladies-in-waiting awoke suddenly from a deep sleep. Everything in the nursery was deathly quiet. So quiet, in fact, that you might have been able to hear a termite munching away on the paneling. The lady-in-waiting looked up and saw a great ugly mouse sitting on the edge of the cradle. Its horrid head was right on the princess's face! Springing to her feet, the lady-in-waiting screamed a scream of terror.

In an instant, the entire nursery and all of the guards awoke. Madame Mouse-rinks (for she was indeed the mouse in the cradle) leaped down to the floor and scurried to a corner. The legislative councillors raced after her, but she had already disappeared through a crack in the floor.

Awakened by all of the commotion, Pirlipat began to cry.

"She's alive!" the ladies-in-waiting exclaimed gleefully. But when they looked upon her face, they gasped in horror.

Her once small, golden-haired head was now huge and bloated and sat upon a shrunken body. Her lovely blue eyes were now green and bulging. And her rosebud mouth had been transformed into a large gash that stretched from one ear clear across to the other.

The queen nearly died of sorrow, and the walls of the king's study had to be covered with padding because he banged his head against them over and over, saying, "Oh, what a miserable king am I!"

Of course, the king might have realized at this point that it would have been better to eat his sausages without any meat at all and leave Madame Mouserinks in peace under the stove. But he didn't think of that. Instead, he chose to blame everything on the clockmaker, Christian Elias Drosselmeier, for failing to catch Madame Mouserinks in one of his traps. He issued a decree giving Drosselmeier just four weeks to find a way to make Pirlipat beautiful again. If he failed, he would be executed.

Now, Drosselmeier was a brilliant clockmaker, and he had faith in his craft and his luck. So he did the logical thing and set to work taking Pirlipat apart — unscrewing her hands and feet and carefully examining her insides. Unfortunately, he learned that the bigger she got the more deformed she would become. Disheartened, he carefully put the princess back together again and slumped to the floor beside her cradle, where the king had commanded him to stay.

Time passed, and soon it was the Wednesday of the fourth week. The furious king barged into the nursery, his eyes flashing with anger. "Christian Elias Drosselmeier," he raged. "Cure the princess or prepare for death!"

Drosselmeier wept bitterly, but Princess Pirlipat seemed unfazed. She simply continued to crack nuts, a task that seemed to give her great satisfaction. Gazing upon the ugly Pirlipat, Drosselmeier suddenly realized the solution lay in her nutcracking habit. After her transformation she had cried and cried until, by a strange chance, she got her tiny hands on a nut. She cracked it at once and ate the nut meat, then lay in her cradle quite content with things. From then on her nurses kept plenty of nuts on hand for Princess Pirlipat.

"O natural instinct!" Drosselmeier cried. "O mysterious, eternal connectedness of all things! You have shown me the secret's door. I shall knock on it, and it shall open!"

Drosselmeier asked permission to leave so that he could meet with the court astronomer. Permission was granted, but the clockmaker had to be escorted and heavily guarded. Upon Drosselmeier's arrival the two men embraced and wept together, for they were good friends. Then they retired to secret quarters and began to read books dealing with all kinds of mysterious subjects.

They read and read, and soon night was

upon them. The astronomer consulted the stars and drew up Pirlipat's horoscope. This was not an easy task, for the lines between the stars became tangled and confused. But at last Princess Pirlipat's destiny was clear, as was the manner in which she could be released from her horrible spell.

It was actually surprisingly simple. All the princess had to do was eat the nut meat of the nut Crackatuk.

Now, the Crackatuk was a hard nut. So hard, in fact, that a steam locomotive could drive over it without hurting it in the least. This impossibly hard nut had to be cracked in Pirlipat's presence by the teeth of a young man who had not yet shaved and had never worn boots. Once the young man had cracked the nut, he was required to give it to the princess with his eyes closed. He then had to take seven steps backward without stumbling.

It had taken Drosselmeier and the court astronomer three days and nights to find the solution to Pirlipat's problem. The very day before he was to be executed, Drosselmeier announced the good news to the king. Elated, the king promised Drosselmeier a diamond sword, four shiny medals, and two Sunday suits.

It was then that Drosselmeier confessed he had found the solution but not the actual nut or the young man to crack it. Furthermore, he said, it would be quite difficult to do so.

"In that case, we'll go through with the execution!" the king bellowed.

Fortunately for the trembling Drosselmeier, the king had enjoyed his noon meal that day. Feeling reasonable, he listened to the advice of the good and kind queen. She pointed out that Drosselmeier had, in fact, found a way to break the spell on little Pirlipat.

"Mishmash and nonsense!" the king declared. But after a few long moments he agreed to send Drosselmeier and the court astronomer out to search for the Crackatuk. They could find the young man to crack it, he said, by advertising in local and foreign newspapers.

❧ ❧ ❧

And now Godfather Drosselmeier interrupted the story again. But he promised Fritz and Marie that he would finish it the very next night.

8

The Second Curse

THE lamps had just been lit the follow-
ing evening when Godfather Drosselmeier arrived. Taking a seat, he quickly
resumed the story of the hard nut.

❧ ❧ ❧

Drosselmeier and the court astronomer
traveled far and wide for fifteen long
years. Still they had not found even a
small trace of the Crackatuk.

I could go on for weeks and weeks
about their adventures. But I shall simply
say that Drosselmeier in particular was
terribly homesick for his hometown of
Nuremberg.

"O Nuremberg, Nuremberg, exquisite

town — where the houses have windows both upstairs and down," he sang sadly.

Hearing his dear friend sound so forlorn, the court astronomer began to weep and moan so loudly that he was heard all over Asia. But he then collected himself and announced that they could look for the Crackatuk anywhere. Why not look for it at home?

"You've got something there," Drosselmeier agreed happily. And so the two men got to their feet and headed straight for Nuremberg. Tired from their journey, they knocked on the door of Drosselmeier's cousin, who was a toymaker and gilder. Drosselmeier told his cousin the long tale of Princess Pirlipat, Madame Mouserinks, and the Crackatuk. He went on to explain his time spent with the King of Dates. How the Prince of Almonds had banned him from his kingdom. And how he had consulted the Natural History Society in Squirreltown to no avail.

When he'd heard the tale, the cousin's eyes opened wide and he threw his cap into the air. "Cousin!" he cried. "You are a made man, for unless I'm mistaken, I have the Crackatuk myself!"

A few moments later, he produced a small box with a medium-sized golden nut inside. How he had come to possess this nut was a story unto itself. But let us say that he watched a wagon ride over it without so much as cracking it. Thinking this quite strange, he bought the nut and dipped it in gold.

The court astronomer examined the nut. Carefully scraping away the gilding, he found the word *Crackatuk* engraved on the shell in Chinese characters. There was excitement and merriment all around. They had found the Crackatuk!

That night, after the two travelers had donned their nightcaps, the astronomer spoke up.

"One piece of good fortune never

comes alone," he said. "I believe we have also found the young man to crack the Crackatuk — your cousin's young son."

Now, the cousin's son was a handsome lad. His smooth chin had never been shaved and he had never worn boots. Just last Christmas he had donned a beautiful red coat with gold trimmings and a shiny sword. Carrying his hat under his arm, he'd sported a fine wig with a pigtail. And in his fancy attire he stood in his father's shop, cracking nuts for the ladies. They called him the handsome nutcracker.

The astronomer set to work making the lad's chart. And by morning he was certain that the boy was indeed the one.

"But there are two things we must do," the astronomer said. "First, you must make him a sturdy wooden pigtail. It must connect to his lower jaw so that a tug on one moves the other. And second, when we get back to the castle, we must hide the fact that we have brought the young man who will crack the Crackatuk. He must remain hidden until several others have broken their teeth trying to crack it. For then the king will promise his daughter's hand and the crown to the one who succeeds."

The toymaker was thrilled that his son was going to become a prince, so much so that he handed the boy over to Drosselmeier altogether.

Drosselmeier built a very sturdy pigtail indeed, which worked splendidly. The boy could crack the hardest peach pits with ease.

Soon it was time for the nut-cracking to take place. Young men came from far and wide — and tried not to gasp when they saw the hideous princess. Her tiny body could barely support her huge, ugly head. And underneath her gash of a mouth had sprouted a stringy white beard.

One bare-faced, bootless traveler after another stepped forward and tried to crack the nut. Each broke his jaw without helping the princess even a tiny bit. As they were carried away to the dentist, they all called out, "Oh, that *was* a hard nut!"

Full of despair, the king promised his daughter and his kingdom to the lad who could crack the Crackatuk. And so young Drosselmeier stepped forward.

The princess gazed at the young lad. "Oh, I hope it is he who cracks the nut and becomes my husband!" she cried.

The lad politely saluted the king and queen. He then took the nut, put it between his teeth, and — *crack, crack!* — broke the shell into many pieces. He carefully removed the last few pieces of husk from the nut meat, then closed his eyes and handed it to the princess.

No sooner had the kernel been chewed and swallowed than the princess again became a beauty to behold. Her face was lily-white, her lips rose-red, and her hair formed delicate golden curls.

Drums beat and trumpets blared. The populace rejoiced. The king gleefully danced about on one foot. The queen, who had fainted from joy and relief, had to be rubbed with perfume.

The young Drosselmeier, however, still had to take his seven steps backward. Trying to remain calm in spite of the excitement, he began. One, two, three —

He was just putting his foot down for the seventh time when Madame Mouserinks squeezed up through the floor with a terrible squeak. The lad stumbled and nearly fell.

Within moments, the handsome boy was transformed into a hideous creature. His giant head and torso became much too large for his shrunken legs. His eyes bugged out and his mouth yawned from

one side of his head to the other. His pigtail was gone, and in its place was a
wooden cloak that moved his jaw.

Drosselmeier and the court astronomer
stared at the boy in horror. Then they saw
Madame Mouserinks on the floor. The
boy had squashed her neck and she would
soon be dead. But with her last gasps of
breath she squeaked out another spell:

"Oh Crackatuk, Crackatuk,
Because of you I must die.
But the Nutcracker, you see,
Soon will follow me.
My beloved son with seven crowns,
Will quickly bring Nutcracker down.
His mother's death he will repay,
Beware, beware, beware that day."

The curse ended, and Madame Mouserinks died. After the mouse's body was
carried out by the court stovekeeper, the

princess reminded the king of his promise. But when she looked upon the now-ugly boy, she raised her hands to her face in horror.

"Take the horrid Nutcracker away!" she cried.

Before he could protest, Nutcracker was seized and removed from the castle. The king was enraged by the idea that a Nutcracker could become his son-in-law. He blamed everything on the court astronomer and the clockmaker and had them banished from the kingdom.

The court astronomer consulted his charts and made some interesting discoveries. In spite of his unfortunate looks, the nutcracking boy would still become a prince and a king. Breaking Madame Mouserinks's spell would be more difficult. A lady would need to fall in love with him in spite of his awful appearance, and he would have to defeat the seven-headed

Mouse King. Once those feats were accomplished, he would become a handsome lad once again.

❧❧ ❧❧ ❧❧

Godfather Drosselmeier cleared his throat. "That is the story of the hard nut, children," he said. "And now you know where the expression 'that was a hard nut to crack' comes from and also why nutcrackers are so ugly."

Marie thought that Princess Pirlipat was horrible and ungrateful. But Fritz was more concerned with Nutcracker. If he was worth his salt, he would fight the King of Mice right away and get his good looks back.

9

Uncle and Nephew

IF you have ever cut yourself on glass, you know how awful such wounds are. They take a very long time to heal. Marie had to stay in bed for many, many days because she was too weak to get up.

Finally, though, she was well enough to play with her lovely Christmas gifts again. The glass panel of the toy cabinet had been repaired, and there were new toys and dolls and houses. But Marie was happiest to see her beloved Nutcracker standing on the second shelf. He smiled broadly at her with his shiny mended teeth.

As she gazed at her Nutcracker, Marie remembered the story Godfather Drossel-

meier had told her. It was all about Nutcracker and Madame Mouserinks. Marie
knew now that Nutcracker was Godfather
Drosselmeier's nephew. For during the
story it had been obvious that the clockmaker was Godfather Drosselmeier himself.

"Why didn't your uncle help you?"
Marie asked Nutcracker, for the battle
Marie had witnessed on Christmas Eve
was most certainly over Nutcracker's
rightful crown and kingdom. Weren't the
dolls and toys Nutcracker's subjects? He
was destined to become a king, after all.

Marie stared at the toy cabinet, expect-
ing to see the toys and dolls come alive.
But they were silent, lifeless, and unmov-
ing.

"It's the curse of Madame Mouserinks,"
Marie said firmly. "But it doesn't matter,"
she told Nutcracker. "I know you can understand me, even if you don't answer.
You know that I love you and will help you

in whatever way I can. And when we need Godfather Drosselmeier's expert assistance, I will ask him for it."

Nutcracker still did not move, but Marie thought she heard a sigh escape from his lips. Then a bell-like whisper came through the glass panes.

"Marie, sweet Marie,
Angel of mine,
If thou saveth me,
I will be thine."

Marie felt a shiver run up her spine, but she was very pleased.

Before long it was evening. Marie's family came in with Godfather Drosselmeier, and soon they were all having tea around a cozy table. Marie pulled a chair up to Godfather Drosselmeier's feet and looked up at him, her blue eyes wide.

"Godfather, I know that Nutcracker is your nephew from Nuremberg. He is a king and a prince, just as the court astronomer said he would be. But he is at war with the horrible Mouse King. Why don't you help him?"

Then Marie told everyone at the table the story of the battle she had witnessed.

"It's not true!" Fritz cried. "My soldiers are not such cowards. I wouldn't waste my time commanding them if they were!"

Dr. Stahlbaum shook his head. "Where do you get such crazy ideas, child?"

"From her lively imagination," replied her mother. "Or perhaps she dreamed it when she was ill in bed."

Only Godfather Drosselmeier was silent. Then he lifted Marie onto his lap. "You are a very lucky girl," he said softly. "Luckier than the rest of us here. You have the chance to be a princess, like Pirlipat, and reign over a beautiful land. But you shall suffer if you befriend the ugly Nutcracker, for the King of Mice will always be waiting for him. There is nothing I can do to help Nutcracker — only you can save him. So be faithful and true."

Marie did not understand what her godfather meant, and neither did the others. In fact, the confusing speech made her father reach for Godfather Drosselmeier's pulse. "You seem to be congested in the head," he said.

10

Victory

NOT long after that, Marie was awakened in the dead of night. A strange noise was coming from the corner of her room — a sort of skittering. Moments later, a horrible squeak filled the air.

"Oh, my!" Marie cried. "Here come those terrible mice again!"

Indeed, the King of Mice was squeezing himself up through a hole in the wall. Marie was so horrified that she could not speak. The Mouse King scurried around the room, then leaped onto the table beside her bed.

"Hee-hee-hee-hee," he cried. "Give me your candy. Marzipan, gingerbread, sugar balls, too. And if you don't, Nutcracker I'll chew!"

The King of Mice gnashed his pointy teeth together, then disappeared through the wall.

Marie shivered in fear. The next morning she was still pale as a ghost. She longed to tell her mother and sister what had happened, but she knew no one would believe her. Still, she laid out all of her sweets at the bottom of the toy cabinet before she went to sleep that night.

The next morning, Mrs. Stahlbaum saw the mess in the parlor.

"I have no idea how mice are getting into the parlor," she said. "They've eaten up all your candy, Marie." Indeed, the Mouse King had gobbled up all of Marie's sweets — except the marzipan. He apparently didn't like marzipan, for he only chewed the edges and scattered the rest across the floor.

Marie was only a little bit sad about giving up her candy. She took heart in the fact that Nutcracker was safe and sound. But she was truly terrified when she heard another horrible squeak next to her ear that very night.

"Give me your sugar dolls," the Mouse King piped. "Oh, yes, you must. Or else I will chew Nutcracker to dust!"

Again Marie longed to confide everything to her mother and sister, or at the very least to her brother, Fritz. She had a lovely collection of sugar dolls and she was very fond of them. There was the little shepherd and his flock of sheep, the handsome men and women in fancy clothes, three dancers, and the farmer, his wife, and their precious little baby.

"Ah!" she cried as she looked over her sugar dolls. "I will give them all up to help you," she told Nutcracker. "But it is very difficult."

Nutcracker only stared at her, but his

eyes were full of sadness. So that night Marie set all of her sugar figures in front of the cabinet.

It was much the same the next morning. "This is awful," Marie's mother said. "Poor Marie's sugar figures are all chewed and eaten."

Marie's eyes were bright with tears. But again she took heart in the fact that Nutcracker was safe, and she was soon smiling once more.

"We need a cat to take care of that mouse," Fritz announced. "The baker downstairs has a big gray one who is very clever. I wish I could walk on the edge of the roof like he can."

Louise scowled. "Please, no cats in the house," she said, for she disliked cats immensely.

"Perhaps we could set a trap for him," Dr. Stahlbaum said. "Do we have a mousetrap?"

"Godfather Drosselmeier will make us

one!" Fritz cried. "After all, he invented them himself!"

Everyone had a good laugh at that. And sure enough, Godfather Drosselmeier sent over an excellent mousetrap that very afternoon.

But oh, how awful it was for Marie that night! Something cold as ice crept up her arm. Something rough and foul lay on her cheek. And then the Mouse King was sitting right on her shoulder! Bloodred foam oozed out of all seven of his mouths.

Grinding and gnashing his teeth, he said, "Hiss, hiss, I know of the trap. I won't venture there — mouse beware! And now for your dresses, your laces, your books. Give them to me, or take one last look. For Nutcracker will perish, die by my teeth. I'll chew him to pieces, and leave you in grief!"

Marie nearly burst into tears right then and there but managed to contain herself.

And as soon as it was light, she hurried to the toy cabinet.

"Oh, my good and kind Mr. Drosselmeier," she sobbed to Nutcracker. "I am such an unfortunate girl! For even if I give up my books and dresses, the King of Mice will be back to ask for more. And when I have nothing left, he'll most certainly want to eat me!"

As she spoke these words, Marie noticed a spot of blood on Nutcracker's neck. It was from the terrible Christmas Eve battle. Marie hadn't held Nutcracker in some time — ever since she'd found out that he was actually Godfather Drosselmeier's nephew. But now she carefully took Nutcracker out of the cabinet and began to rub off the blood with her handkerchief. As she did so, Nutcracker began to grow warm in her hand. Then he moved and spoke!

"Ah, my dear, sweet Marie," he said. "I

am indebted to you for all you have done. But don't sacrifice any more of your toys or your dresses. Instead, get me a sword of my own. Then I will manage the rest —"

Nutcracker broke off, becoming lifeless once again. Marie, however, was filled with joy. Now she knew how to save Nutcracker! But where would she find a sword?

There was only one person to ask — her brother, Fritz. So that night, after her parents had gone out, she sat with him in front of the toy cabinet and told him everything.

Fritz was most concerned about his soldiers and their performance at the end of the battle. They had fled the scene and acted like cowards, and this upset him greatly. Fritz asked Marie again if this was really true. When she told him that it was, he plucked the feathers from their soldiers' caps and forbade them from marching.

74

"As for a sword, I have one here," he said. He borrowed a sharp saber from a retired colonel and fastened it to Nutcracker's side. Then Marie and Fritz both went to bed.

Just after midnight, Marie heard strange and awful sounds in the parlor. There was rustling and clanging and then a horrible, bloodcurdling *squeeeeak*.

"The King of Mice!" Marie shouted, leaping out of bed. All was silent . . . until a soft tapping echoed on her bedroom door.

"Please open the door, Marie," came a voice. "Do not be alarmed. I bring joyous news!"

Marie hurriedly put on her bathrobe and opened the door. It was Nutcracker. His sword was covered in blood, and he carried the seven jeweled crowns of the Mouse King.

"Thank you, dear lady, for giving me the courage and strength to fight the King of

Mice. He now lies dying in a pool of his own blood. Please accept this gift from me, your ever-faithful knight."

He removed the crowns from his arm and handed them to Marie. Marie smiled.

"And now," Nutcracker continued, "if you would only follow me a short way. I have beautiful and enchanting things to show you."

The Land of Toys

MARIE did not hesitate to go with Nutcracker, for she knew him to be a trusted friend.

"I will follow you," she said. "But we cannot go too far, for I have not yet slept tonight."

Nutcracker promised to take the shortest route and led her to the large, old wardrobe. The door hung open, which surprised Marie, since it was always kept closed. Nutcracker climbed nimbly up the sleeve of Marie's father's fancy winter coat. He pulled on a tassel hanging near the collar, and a ladder tumbled down through the sleeve, which suddenly seemed very big.

"Now, if you will step up the ladder," Nutcracker said.

Marie obliged and was soon poking her head out through the neck. As she did so, a dazzling light streamed down on her. She was suddenly standing in a sweet-smelling meadow sparkling with light.

"This is Candy Mead," Nutcracker explained. "But soon we will pass under that arch."

Marie looked up and saw a glorious archway just ahead. It was made of baked almonds and raisins! At the top of the arch was a balcony. Six monkeys in red suits sat on it, playing music on brass instruments. The music was so lovely that Marie barely noticed that she was walking on a path of hard candy!

"It is so wonderful here!" Marie cried in delight.

"This is Christmas Wood," Nutcracker explained. He clapped his hands, and several shepherds appeared. They were so white that Marie thought they might be made of sugar. They brought in a reclining chair and invited Marie to have a seat. As soon as she did, they began to dance a pretty ballet. When they were done, they all disappeared.

"I apologize for the poor dancing style," Nutcracker said. "Those dancers are part of a music box and can only do the same movements over and over again. But shall we continue?"

Marie stood and followed Nutcracker. They walked along a babbling brook that filled the air with a wonderful smell.

"This is Orange Brook," Nutcracker said. "It is quite pleasant, but not as spectacular as Lemonade River. Both of these waters fall into the Almond-milk Sea."

They walked farther, and Marie caught a glimpse of a yellow river as it tumbled into a giant cream-colored sea. Just a little ways downstream, they came upon a charming village. The buildings were all dark brown with golden roofs.

"That is Gingertown on Honey River," Nutcracker said, pointing. "We won't visit, because everyone who lives there always has a toothache."

The next little town had shimmering buildings of all different colors. There was quite a hubbub in the town center, where busy people were unloading bars of chocolate from a dozen wagons.

"This is Candy Village," Nutcracker explained. "The people are busy unpacking a shipment from the King of Chocolate. They've been receiving threats from the Prince of Flies, and the King has sent materials to strengthen and protect their houses. But we are losing time seeing the country. We must go on to the capital!"

Nutcracker hurried now, leading the way down the path. Soon the scent of roses filled the air, and everything around them was covered in a soft pink hue. Lapping the ground in front of them was a giant rose-colored lake! The lake seemed to get wider and wider as Marie gazed at it. And swimming across its surface were beautiful white swans with gold collars.

"Oh!" Marie cried. "This must be the lake Godfather Drosselmeier once told me about."

Nutcracker smiled. "Let's sail across its rosy waters to the capital!"

12

The Capital

NUTCRACKER clapped his little hands. Within moments a lovely, shell-shaped boat appeared on top of the cresting waves. Made of colorful, glittering stones, it was pulled by a pair of dolphins. As soon as Marie and Nutcracker climbed inside, the boat began to cross Rose Lake. Filled with wonder, Marie watched the waves — each of which seemed to hold the face of a smiling girl.

"Look!" she cried, clapping her hands together. "It's Princess Pirlipat, smiling at me so sweetly."

Nutcracker sighed sadly and shook his head. "That is not Princess Pirlipat, dear

Marie, but your own self smiling up at you."

Marie was ashamed of her foolishness and closed her eyes tightly. When she opened them again she was standing in a beautiful, glittering grove. The trees were all sorts of strange colors and the fruit smelled like perfume.

"Here we are in Marmalade Grove," Nutcracker said. "And just ahead lies the capital."

Marie looked up and gasped, for the capital was the most beautiful city she had ever seen. The walls and towers of the buildings were all different colors. Instead of roofs, sparkling spires and crowns topped the structures.

As they passed the macaroon and sugared-fruit gate, a little man in a brocade suit embraced Nutcracker tightly.

"Welcome, dear prince," he cried. "Welcome to Confection City!"

Marie was surprised to see such a well-dressed man call Nutcracker a prince, but she quickly forgot it as she took in the excitement around her. There was so much singing, dancing, and celebrating going on that she had to ask Nutcracker what it all meant.

"Oh, sweet Marie," Nutcracker replied. "Confection City is a bustling metropolis. It is like this all the time. Let's just go a little farther."

Soon they came to the main marketplace. Marie gasped at the sight. The houses were constructed of delicately carved sugar, and in the center was a giant cake. Fountains surrounded the cake, spewing lemonade and orangeade into the air. And the canals running alongside the paths were full of delicious creams. But more wonderful than all of this were the people in the marketplace. They danced and sang, laughed and played. There were people of all shapes and sizes and colors. Indeed, they seemed to come from all over the world.

One corner of the marketplace seemed noisier than the others. An important Mongolian was being carried along in a special carrier, escorted by several hundred followers. Not far away, five hundred members of the Fishermen's Association were attending their annual festival. And as if that were not enough, the Sultan of Turkey chose that moment to ride across the square with three thousand soldiers.

It was a large marketplace, but not large enough for all of this to occur at the same moment. Things got crowded and confused, and soon there were pushing, shoving, and cries of pain.

The man who had embraced Nutcracker just inside the macaroon gate climbed to the top of a spire. "Pastry cook! Pastry cook! Pastry cook!" he shouted.

In an instant, the crowd quieted. The people untangled themselves, brushed themselves off, and went on their way.

"Why did that man call out 'pastry cook'?" Marie asked.

"Ah," Nutcracker replied thoughtfully. "In Confection City, pastry cook refers to a strange and terrible power that can do whatever it wishes with people. The citizens live in such fear of pastry cook that just mentioning it will put an end to any scuffle."

By then Marie was only half listening to Nutcracker, for she had seen a beautiful castle up ahead, bathed in a rose-colored glow. It had a hundred sparkling towers. Scattered on its walls were glorious bouquets of violets, tulips, and carnations. And the giant dome in the center of the building was covered in thousands of glittering stars.

Marie was awestruck by this magic

palace, yet she noticed that part of one of the tower spires had been broken off.

"This beautiful castle was recently under attack," Nutcracker explained. "A terrible and hungry giant named Sweet Tooth walked by and bit off the top of that tower. He was just about to chew on a large dome when the people of Confection City offered him a quarter of the town instead. The giant ate it all, then stopped and gorged himself at Marmalade Grove. His belly full, he went on his way, leaving the good citizens in peace."

Nutcracker's story was interrupted when soft music filled the air. The castle gates opened and twelve pages made of precious stones and gold stepped out. They carried whole cloves, which were lit like torches. Behind the pages came four ladies about the size of Marie's Mistress Clara. They were so beautiful and dressed in such finery that Marie knew at once they had to be princesses. The ladies hugged Nutcracker warmly.

"Oh, dear brother!" they cried. "Beloved prince!"

Nutcracker embraced his sisters, his eyes overflowing with tears. Then he wiped them away and took Marie's hand.

"This is Marie Stahlbaum," he said. "She has saved my life. Had she not thrown her shoe, sacrificed her treasured belongings, or given me a sword, I would have been bitten to death by the horrid King of Mice. And now I ask you, can Princess Pirlipat compare with the kind and virtuous Marie?"

"No!" cried the princesses. They hugged Marie with tears in their eyes, grateful for her strength and good deeds.

Then Nutcracker and Marie were led into a castle hall made of sparkling crystal. Quaint little sofas and chairs and writing tables made of carved cedarwood furnished the hall. While Marie and Nut-cracker rested in two cozy chairs, the princesses prepared a banquet in their honor.

Marie watched the princesses work. They got out tiny cups and porcelain dishes and golden spoons and knives and forks. Then they began to prepare delicious-looking fruits and sugar cakes. They gently squeezed the fruit, grated the spices, and rubbed the skin off the almonds.

Marie admired their work, for the princesses clearly knew a great deal about cooking. But she felt a little envious and wanted to do some of the preparation herself.

One of the princesses seemed to read Marie's mind, for she said, "Sweet friend, would you please pound a bit of this candy?"

Marie beamed and took the mortar and pestle. As she pounded the candy, the sound seemed to make a kind of lilting music. She heard Nutcracker tell the tale of all that had happened. But as he did so, his voice seemed to get farther and farther away. Then she saw a girl who looked quite a bit like herself floating in the clouds, and the princesses and Nutcracker and the pages were there, too. Then the air was filled with a strange buzzing, and Marie was lifted higher and higher and higher.

A Dream Come True

CRASH! Marie tumbled and landed. When she opened her eyes, she was at home in her very own bed! It was morning, and her mother was standing right there in her room.

"You've slept very late this morning, Marie," she said. "Breakfast has been ready for a long time."

Marie, of course, knew exactly what must have happened. Dazed by all the wonderful things she'd seen in the Land of Toys, she had finally fallen asleep in the castle. And someone — perhaps the pages or the princesses — had carried her home and put her to bed.

"Oh, Mother!" Marie cried. "Last night

Nutcracker took me to the most wonderful places!" And she told her mother all about Christmas Wood, Gingertown, Lemonade River, Candy Village, Marmalade Grove, and Confection City.

Mrs. Stahlbaum listened to her daughter, then looked at her quite seriously. "You've had a long and wonderful dream," she said. "But now you must forget all about it."

Marie, of course, knew that it had not been a dream. When she insisted, her mother took her to the toy cabinet and pointed at Nutcracker.

"He is as still and lifeless as ever, you foolish child," she said.

But Marie was not convinced. She knew in her heart that Nutcracker was really young Mr. Drosselmeier from Nuremberg. This caused her parents to laugh at her, and even Fritz called her a silly goose.

Annoyed, Marie went to her room and

brought out the sparkling Mouse King crowns. Her parents stared at them in amazement, for they were so intricate and beautiful that they could not have been made by human hands.

"Where did you get them?" her father asked.

Marie told her family over and over that her tale was true, and still they did not believe her. Finally, Marie was reduced to tears. "I can only tell you the truth!" she sobbed.

Just then the door opened, and Godfather Drosselmeier appeared. "But why is my little Marie crying?" he asked. Dr. Stahlbaum told him what had happened, and Godfather Drosselmeier waved his hand in the air.

"Mishmash and nonsense!" he said. "These are the crowns I used to wear on my watch chains. I gave them to Marie on her second birthday. Do you mean to tell me you don't remember?"

None of the Stahlbaums, who all had very good memories, remembered anything of the sort.

Marie stood before her godfather and gazed into his eyes. "Tell them, tell them that Nutcracker is your nephew. Tell them that he gave me the crowns," she begged.

Godfather Drosselmeier looked down at Marie with a blank stare. "Mishmash and nonsense!" he declared.

Then Dr. Stahlbaum took Marie firmly by the shoulders and demanded that she forget all about the Nutcracker. "If I hear another word about his being your godfather's nephew, I'm going to throw him — and the rest of your toys — out the window," he scolded.

From then on Marie was silent. But of course she remembered everything, and she thought about Nutcracker and his enchanted kingdom all the time. Her family complained that she had become a daydreamer, but what was Marie to do?

Not long after that, Godfather Drossel-meier came to repair one of the clocks in the Stahlbaum house. Marie sat in the parlor, daydreaming and gazing at Nut-cracker. Then, all of a sudden, she spoke aloud.

"Dear Mr. Drosselmeier," she said. "If you were really alive, I would never de-spise you because you had turned ugly for me. Not like Princess Pirlipat."

"Mishmash and nonsense!" Godfather Drosselmeier cried. But as the words came out of his mouth, there was a huge bang and a jolt. Right then and there Marie fainted and fell out of her chair. When she came back to her senses, her mother was standing over her.

"What is a big girl like you doing falling out of a chair?" she asked. "We have a guest — Godfather Drosselmeier's nephew from Nuremberg. Let's show him our best behavior."

Marie looked up and saw Godfather

Drosselmeier, who was smiling broadly. Standing next to him was a handsome young man. He wore a red jacket trimmed with gold and white stockings and shoes. A large pigtail hung down his back, and the sword he carried was covered in jewels.

The young man was ever so polite, and he brought Marie several sugar dolls and sweets, just like the ones that had been eaten by the Mouse King. At the dinner table the young man cracked nuts for the whole family, pulling on his pigtail each time a nut was put into his mouth. Marie noticed that even the shells of the hardest nuts cracked with ease.

Marie was quite shy around the handsome young man. And when he asked her to go with him to the toy cabinet in the parlor, her face grew red. But her parents and Godfather Drosselmeier had no objections.

"Play nicely," Godfather Drosselmeier said with a wave of his hand.

No sooner did they reach the toy cabinet than the young Drosselmeier bent down on one knee.

"Ah, my beloved Marie," he began. "Here I am, the man whose life you saved in this exact spot. You were kind enough to tell me that you would never despise me for turning ugly to free you from a spell. When you said those words, I ceased to be a wooden nutcracker. Instead, I am my regular, not too ugly self! And now I ask you to become my queen and reign with me in Marzipan Castle, for I am king there now."

Marie could hardly believe her ears. She helped Nutcracker to his feet. "Mr. Drosselmeier," she replied, "you are a kind and good gentleman, and you reign over a land of charming and wonderful people. I would be thrilled to be your queen."

At that moment they became formally engaged. And a year and a day later, Nutcracker picked Marie up in a golden carriage pulled by silver horses. Thousands of beautiful pearl-and-diamond dolls danced at their wedding, which was a glorious celebration.

To this day, Marie is queen of the enchanted land made up of sweet and sparkling buildings, forests, and people. Her world is the most beautiful of all, and anyone who believes can see it.